My Aunt Mary Went Shopping

by Roger Hall

Illustrated by

Trevor Pye

READ BY READING

Ashton Scholastic

Auckland   Sydney   New York   London   Toronto

First published 1991

Ashton Scholastic Limited
Private Bag 1, Penrose, Auckland, New Zealand.

Ashton Scholastic Pty Ltd
PO Box 579, Gosford, NSW 2250, Australia.

Scholastic Inc.
730 Broadway, New York, NY 10003, USA.

Scholastic Canada Ltd
123 Newkirk Road, Richmond Hill, Ontario L4C 3G5, Canada.

Scholastic Publications Ltd
Marlborough House, Holly Walk, Leamington Spa, Warwickshire
CV32 4LS, England.

National Library of New Zealand
Cataloguing-in-Publication data

Hall, Roger, 1939 -
    My Aunt Mary went shopping / by Roger Hall ; illustrated by
Trevor Pye. Auckland, N.Z. : Ashton Scholastic, 1991.
    1 v. (Read by reading)
    ISBN 1-86943-040-9
    1. Readers (Elementary) I. Title. II. Series: Read by reading
series.
    428.6 (823.2)

987654321   12345678/9

Typeset by Rennies Illustrations Ltd
Printed in Malaysia by SRM Productions Services Sdn. Bhd.

My Aunt Mary went shopping
and she bought a giraffe.

My Aunt Mary went shopping
and she bought a giraffe,
and a scarf for the giraffe.

My Aunt Mary went shopping and she bought
a giraffe, a scarf for the giraffe,
and a goat.

My Aunt Mary went shopping and she bought
a giraffe, a scarf for the giraffe,
a goat,
and a coat for the goat.

My Aunt Mary went shopping and she bought
a giraffe, a scarf for the giraffe,
a goat, a coat for the goat,
and some yaks.

My Aunt Mary went shopping and she bought
a giraffe, a scarf for the giraffe,
a goat, a coat for the goat,
some yaks,
and some slacks for the yaks.

My Aunt Mary went shopping and she bought
a giraffe, a scarf for the giraffe,
a goat, a coat for the goat,
some yaks, some slacks for the yaks,
and a rat.

My Aunt Mary went shopping and she bought
a giraffe, a scarf for the giraffe,
a goat, a coat for the goat,
some yaks, some slacks for the yaks,
a rat,
and a hat for the rat.

My Aunt Mary went shopping and she bought
a giraffe, a scarf for the giraffe,
a goat, a coat for the goat,
some yaks, some slacks for the yaks,
a rat, a hat for the rat,
and some pigs.

My Aunt Mary went shopping and she bought
a giraffe, a scarf for the giraffe,
a goat, a coat for the goat,
some yaks, some slacks for the yaks,
a rat, a hat for the rat,
some pigs,
and some wigs for the pigs.

13

My Aunt Mary went shopping and she bought
a giraffe, a scarf for the giraffe,
a goat, a coat for the goat,
some yaks, some slacks for the yaks,
a rat, a hat for the rat,
some pigs, some wigs for the pigs,
and some llamas.

My Aunt Mary went shopping and she bought
a giraffe, a scarf for the giraffe,
a goat, a coat for the goat,
some yaks, some slacks for the yaks,
a rat, a hat for the rat,
some pigs, some wigs for the pigs,

some llamas,
and some pyjamas for the llamas.

Then they all went home for dinner.

What a noise! What a fuss! What an uproar!

The giraffe wanted a staff not a scarf.
The goat wanted a boat not a coat.
The yaks wanted snacks not slacks.
The rat wanted a mat not a hat.
The pigs wanted figs not wigs.

But luckily . . .

very luckily . . .

the llamas loved their pyjamas.